GHOST SCOUTS

Hullabaloo at Camp Croak!

taylor dolan

GUPPY
BOOKS

Thank you to my quarantine buddies, near and far.
Brandon, you've brought me so many laughs.
Junli, thank you for never judging my shopping habits.
Also, I adore you.
Chloe, your joy and puppy pictures are life.

GHOST SCOUTS: Hullabaloo at Camp Croak!
is a GUPPY BOOK

First published in the UK in 2021 by
Guppy Books
Brackenhill
Cotswold Road
Oxford OX2 9JG

Text and illustrations © Taylor Dolan, 2021
Cover and insides designed by Ness Wood

978-1-913101-13-8

1 3 5 7 9 10 8 6 4 2

The rights of Taylor Dolan to be identified as the author and illustrator of this
work have been asserted in accordance with the Copyright, Designs
and Patents Act 1988.

Papers used by Guppy Books are from well-managed forests
and other responsible sources.

MIX
Paper from
responsible sources
FSC
www.fsc.org   FSC™ C130176

GUPPY PUBLISHING LTD Reg. No. 11565833

A CIP catalogue record for this book is available from the British Library.

Typeset in 15/26pt ITC Clearface by Falcon Oast Graphic Art Ltd.
Printed and bound by Grafostil, Slovenia.

To my marvellous mom and delightful dad,
I told you I would dedicate a book
to you one day. Well, this is it!
Soak it up while you can;
the next one is going to be to the Fab Five.
Mark my words.

chapter one

A QUICK TIP
ABOUT WISHES

If I showed up at your front door, looked you square in the eye and said, "Whatever you do next, don't think about giant tap dancing lizard unicorns," we both know,

 1

no matter how hard you tried, those Liz-a-corns would shuffleflap across your brain quicker than a Broadway chorus.

So, I'm super-duper aware that when I say, "WISHES ARE DANGEROUS, don't make them," you're automatically gonna try anyways. But I beg of you, with all my little heart: DO. NOT. DO. IT.

I know, I know – in movies, good people make good wishes and get good things. Some twinkly fairy spends his time waiting for a wish to be made, so he can dole out unbreakable glass shoes and kissable amphibians. But this *ain't* a movie.

Emmy LouLou's Cousin Chouteau (that's '*Shoe-toe*' for those of y'all from out of town) used to spit out wishes like warm mouthwash. More than anything, he wanted to compete in the Great

Patriotic American Dog Show. Sad part was, these stuffy ol' pageants don't appreciate the beauty of a plus-sized pup. Rude. So he would wish *every day* that he could magically lose thirteen kilos.

And then one day, he did.

Cousin Chouteau was minding his own business, making wishes and pancakes, when Little Red herself, the Great Scourge of the North American werewolf population, showed up with a pair of hair clippers.

Now, how much do you think
all that fuzz weighed? That's right.
Thirteen. Kilos.

You see, on a normal unmagical
day, you can squeeze out any kind of
wish you want and things might not
turn out too bad. But if that same wish
lingers on a day buzzing with magic,
and a Wishwind is summoned . . . Well
now, you better hope you chose your
wish words carefully.

I'm only telling all y'all this cause
I didn't know.

None of us did until it was way
too late.

Chapter two

BEE PREPARED

"One, two, three, eyes on me!" chuckled Miss Parsleigh over the screeching of the cicadas as we circled up outside one fine morning. "Oh, hey now, hold your horses, Mary, that was a figure of speech. I don't actually *want* your eyeballs. Feel free to keep them in your heads for now. Anywhoodle, we have ourselves a very important choice to make today!"

I wanted to focus on her words, and be respectful or whatever, but oh my gods! The swamp was a literal oven, and I felt like a poor banana nut muffin left in to cook for too long. Even my ears were sweaty!

"Visitors' Weekend is only one day away, and this . . ." Miss Sage raised her impressive eyebrows at us. "This *thisness* is much too

clean." She jabbed her perfectly sharpened nails at our swampy ol' Camp Croak.

"We have ourselves two options," said Miss Rosemarie, patting a tablecloth covering something secret. A secret that was moving . . . "Option A: work ourselves to the bone creepifying our beloved Camp Croak, probably pass out from heatstroke and have to skip all the badges we had planned for this afternoon. Or Option B: five minutes of . . . the Bumblebee!"

I could feel my brain gears clunking into action. I know options. Options are when people say, "Do you want

a hot dog or a corn dog for lunch?"
Options are when you get up in the
morning and decide to put on your
favourite smelly shirt out of the
laundry instead of the clean one in
your drawer. Options are NOT boring
clean-up duty or being bee stung!

I looked over at my
pals expecting
to see Emmy
LouLou
showing
a few bald
patches or
dropping a
whisker or two

like she does sometimes when she's stressing. Nope indeedy, none of that. Instead she was giggling like a fiend and high-fiving Bébé.

"BumbleBEE! BumbleBEE! BumbleBEE!" my wicked friends chanted. Maybe skeletons, werewolves, ghosts and zombies don't feel bee stings. But my soft squishy people-skin sure does!

"BUMBLEBEE IT IS!" whooped the Sisters, in merry agreement. And with the flair of that sparkly lady on game shows, they flipped away the tablecloth.

Please, sweet baby Jesus, not a box of bees. Anything, but a box of bees . . .

chapter three

THE CLEAN-UP SONG

Well, it was not a box of bees. It was a buzzing violin covered in swarming shaking bees and a sticky jar of honey. I have to say, I did not see that one coming.

"The time is now! Scoot your

boots!" clapped Miss Parsleigh before
prying off the jar lid and gulping down
a dollop of gorgeous glowing honey.

Suddenly, everybody else was

rushing to get their hands, paws and claws on some too. Bears waking up from their winter snooze couldn't chug down honey faster than these goobers.

The Sisters picked up their dangerous violin and played one long note. And as they dragged that bowstring, something mighty strange began to happen. My friends started

speeding up. Their bodies buzzed.
Some magic between the honey and
the violin music was making them
move in fast-forward.

"LexieLexieLexie,YouHavetoEatThe-
HoneyQuickFastNow!" blurted out
Emmy LouLou.

"LadiesandGentlefolk,IGiveYouthe-

FlightoftheBumblebee!" zoomed Miss Rosemarie, beaming from ear to ear as she leaned into her violin.

"AsTheySay,StartYourEngines!" hallooed Mary.

"FasterFasterFaster,Lexie,ISaid Faster!" zipped Bébé.

I squinted real close at the bees perched on this violin of theirs. Much to my surprise, they didn't seem bothered by all the loud noise and honey eating. In fact, some of them were tapping their toes in a little happy dance.

So I dipped my finger into the pot and scooped out some for myself.

And that's when the Sisters started really playing. Sawing and swiping their bow across the strings with such force, I thought the horsehair was going to shred right up. Like a puppet on a string, my heartbeat followed the dizzying music. With all the newfound fastness of a cheetah on a snack hunt, everyone got to work.

ZOOM!

I put up some new cobwebs.

ZOOM!
ZOOM!

I tidied up the carnivorous vegetable

cages.

ZOOM!
ZOOM!
ZOOM!

I scrub-a-dubbed Kraken Dave's back.

All in under THIRTY SECONDS.

And I wasn't the only one getting things done. In fact, we broke SEVEN household cleaning World Records that day, that's how dang speedy we were.

When the Sisters played their final note, only five minutes later, Camp Croak was looking her very bestest.

chapter four
TIME TO SHINE

You would think that after all that fast-forward chore stuff, we would be too tired for any afternoon fun. BOOM! Think again! I'VE NEVER FELT MORE ALIVE! This must be what parents feel like when they

drink three cups of black coffee in the
morning . . .

We pulled out the mega-chart of
Ghost Scout badges and got to picking.
Every single option was a million
times better than those nasty ones we
earned when Scoutmaster Vile was in
charge . . .

First up, Sweet
Boo chose the
First Aid badge.
We invited a few
local zombies in need
of pampering to help us
with this one.

Of course, Bébé requested the Knot Tying badge.

Followed by Emmy
LouLou's surprise pick –
the Marksmanship badge.

And last but not least, Mary reminded us that balancing on crutches is a tough business on a good day, and squishy swamp mud ain't all that great for your standard wheelchair. So we finished up with a joint pick between the two of us and worked on the nifty Robotics badge.

By the time
the sun
set on our
glorious
swamp,
not even my
excitement about
seeing Grams tomorrow could keep
me awake. I nodded
off with a smile
on my lips and
a snore in my
nose.

me

Grams

chapter five

THE EARLY BIRD GETS THE HUG

Here is how I imagined my morning would go:

Once upon a time, in a swamp where alligators talk and mosquitoes mind their own business, an intelligent and super interesting girl

went to summer camp. She loved her summer camp. But she missed her Grams something fierce.

The little girl was not too worried though, because after weeks of waiting, it was officially Visitors' Weekend! YAY! She woke up extra early that morning just in time to see something totally awesome possum.

Was it a shooting star? Was it a cow with wings? NOPE. It was Grams, flying into camp on the

back of an extra special mechanical bull.

The little girl ran outside to meet her glorious Grams (who smelled like peaches and Sunday nights) and they hugged for ever and ever.

The End. Happily Ever After.

me

chapter six

THE EARLY BIRD DOESN'T EVEN GET THE CORNDOG

*U*gh. Now, here is how my morning ACTUALLY went:

"Cock-a-doodle-y-doo, wakey-wakey eggs and bakey! Your families are here and we are gonna eat all this fine breakfast without y'all!" screamed the Sisters over our crackling cabin speakers.

In a jumble of joy and unbrushed teeth, we jumped out of bed, launched ourselves into our uniforms and booked it to the picnic area.

Soon, everybody had somebody.

Mary was lost in a sea of dad hugs.

Emmy
LouLou
was being
squashed
by her
dad while
he happy-cried
and was being fed by her mom out of
a pile of steaming hot tupperware she
had stashed in her bag. All the while,
Bébé was executing a seriously cool

handshake
with her
dad, the
Baron
Samedi.

Sweet Boo was petting a random swamp cat.

Everybody had somebody. Everybody. All except little old me. Houston, we have a serious big-time problem. Where was Grams?

"Lexie, you look concerned," Mary said when she saw me on my second stress loop of the picnic area. "Don't be. The chances

are high that your Grams, as you call her, is simply running late. Or she is in the hospital and there is nothing you can do about it. You should try relaxing."

I didn't mean to, but I think I gave Mary a little bit of a death glare. Grams was never ever late. Her bedside table had two different alarm clocks just in case the batteries ran out in one of them. I was one hundred percent certain that even a herd of raging cattle couldn't stop her from being here with me.

She is my whole only family, after all. My dad tried to bring me up by himself, but he had too much sadness inside his skin. And my mama? Never met her. All I got is one blurry picture.

So when I say to you with my hand over my heart, that Grams is my everything, you best believe me!

Sometimes, a person just knows things. And with no facts at all, my heart was telling me something was terribly horribly badly wrong with my Grams.

chapter seven

HIT THE NAIL ON THE HEAD, EXCEPT I AM THE NAIL AND NOW MY HEAD REALLY HURTS

"Yoohoo! Helloooo? Is anybody there?" twittered a new voice, chopping through my brain chaos.

Great, just what we needed – a

lost hiker. And on a day when we had double the number of dead people in camp. That'd take some explaining . . .

"I apologize for raising my voice," the stranger smiled, as she stepped out of a patch of hanging moss. "Such a dreadful way to attract attention, but I am here on serious business. I was told that my daughter goes to this camp. Which one of you is my sweet baby . . . Lexie?"

Hold your horses, honey bun – her sweet baby who?! THAT'S MY MOM? SHE IS HERE? RIGHT NOW?

Sweet Boo put herself between me and the stranger, like a protective fishing bobber with tiny sharp teeth.

"Not to be rude," muttered Emmy LouLou, "but that accent of yours ain't quite right, is it? Is it Swedish? Irish? . . . Sw-Irish? How do we know you are who you say you are?"

"Are you really a nun?" broke in Mary. "If you are indeed Lexie's mother, and a high-ranking holy woman, does that make you a mother Mother Superior?"

"And coming back to the mega-elephant in the swamp, IF, and I really mean that big ol' 'IF', you actually are her mama, where in the H-E-double-hockey-sticks you been all these years?" spat Bébé.

The stranger kept her sharply smiling eyes glued on me the whole time they were talking. "You must be my Lexie then. Would you kindly call off your attack dogs? I'm sure they

think they
are being
helpful, but
this is a
private
family
matter.
In fact, I have
a letter from your
grandmother that you
should read." And
she pulled out
a note and
gave it
to me.

lexie,

i have moved to hawaii.
DON'T write back to me;
you are very boring, and
hawaii has cat sanctuaries.
TRUST me, it was an
easy choice. have a nice
life with YOUR MOTHER.
SHE lives in a convent
called 'our lady of perpetual
misery and suffering.' it IS
in the mountains somewhere
cold and BAD.

-grammy gram

chapter eight

DONT JUDGE THE NOTE BY ITS COVER

I stared at the note, hoping that if I looked at it long enough, the words might wiggle around and say something different. Something better. I would have burst into a waterfall of

tears, except . . .

I looked at the letter again. It was in Gram's handwriting alright, but really, y'all, why on God's green earth would she sign it 'GrammyGram'? It's ridiculous, I would never call her that. Sounds like some sort of old lady attempt at a rapper name. Like DJ Hip Replacement or Lady Denturzzz. Something was real fishy. And this here letter  needed some private investigating!

Crying out loud in public is the fastest way to make other people  uncomfortable. So, I threw my hands over my face, and put on my very bestest pretend blubbering voice.

"Don't look at me!" I howled. "I must be alone while I digest this deepest heartbreak. I will be over there, in that clump of bushes. It shall become a sadness zone. There will be tears. And snot. I ask that you respect my wishes and leave me alone in this time of darkness."

With an extra wail, I wiped my nose and threw myself sideways into the bushes.

When I was sure no one had followed me, I flattened the letter and read it again. There was a time, when I was real little, when Grams would put secret notes in my lunch box. If I circled all the capitalized words, there was always a hidden message. I wonder . . .

lexie,

i have moved to hawaii. DON'T write back to me; you are very boring, and hawaii has cat sanctuaries. TRUST me, it was an easy choice. have a nice life with YOUR MOTHER. SHE lives in a convent called 'our lady of perpetual misery and suffering.' it IS in the mountains somewhere cold and BAD

-grammy gram

Holy crow on a stick! I wish Grams were here right now, she would be so proud of me for cracking this code wide open:

DON'T
TRUST
YOUR MOTHER.
SHE
IS
BAD.

chapter nine

AND NOW FOR SOMETHING COMPLETELY DIFFERENT

I poked my head out of the shrubs and was just sneak whistling to get Emmy LouLou's attention when all the sounds of our swamp were cut off with a SNAP.

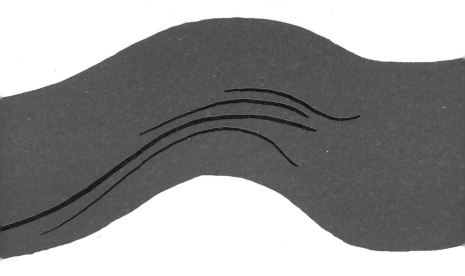

No cicadas hiss singing.

No small talking.

Nothing.

It was like some giant in the sky had pressed a big ol' mute button on our lives. Then, out of all that quiet came a softly hissing wind. The wind had a voice! The voice was so small and soft, it tickled the little peach fuzz on my neck.

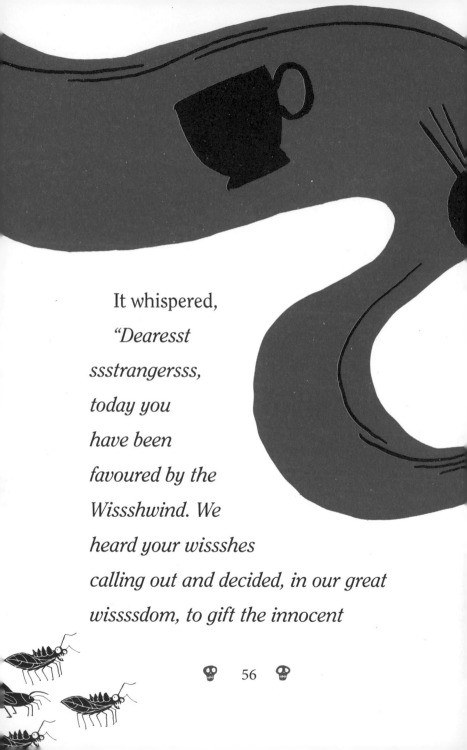

It whispered,
"*Dearesst*
ssstrangersss,
today you
have been
favoured by the
Wissshwind. We
heard your wissshes
calling out and decided, in our great
wissssdom, to gift the innocent

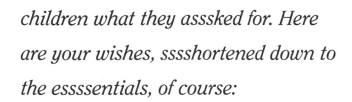

children what they asssked for. Here are your wishes, sssshortened down to the essssentials, of course:

CUP.

TEA.

CATSSSS.

COLD.

AIR. GROW. BIGGER. GRAMSSSS.

Prepare yourselves for greatnessss."

chapter ten

DID I DO THAT?

"**H**ave I missed something?" I mumbled at Miss Sage, who was doing her very best impression of a three-headed deer stuck in headlights. "Why are all y'all ruffled over a few lousy wishes?"

Miss Sage looked around warily.

"Wishwinds are rare beasties and only show up when they are summoned! Somebody made this Wishwind come here today with plans of doing mischief."

"Think of it this way," added my new 'mom', earwigging on our chat. "When the Wishwind said 'CUP. TEA' someone was wishing for a basic cup of tea. Most likely that girl with the big head. The English can't go twenty-four hours without tea or they explode. Just you wait and see."

As if on cue, Mary let out an unholy screech.

"I have made an Earl Grey related error," she sobbed. "I am to blame. It is all my fault."

"Babes, what you talking about, huh?" crooned Bébé, stepping forward to calm her down. "No need to fuss over tea, you just need a nice snuggle. Where have your dads gone off to?"

"There!" Mary screamed, pointing wildly at two small teacups snug in the grass at her feet. Two small teacups exactly where her dads had been standing just seconds before.

Oh my lanta! Nuh-uh. The

Wishwind had taken her nice
normal dads and turned them
into crockery.

"Oh me. Oh my. All right, Mary,
look at me. We can solve this. I'm
sure we have a spell somewhere that
can fix them right up." Miss Parsleigh
scrunched her eyes up, thinking
hard.

"Yes, do your very best to remain
calm. Breathe in through your
nose holes, and out through your
mouth." Miss Sage was trying and not
succeeding to sound like a responsible
adult. "Rosemarie, any ideas?"

"Meow," yelled Miss Rosemarie.

She looked as surprised as we did as, like a teenager with acne, her confused face exploded into a breakout the likes of which no doctor has ever seen. Cause instead of spots and pimples, patches of sleek black fur bloomed across her cheeks and neck. Soon all three of the Sisters were sprouting fur, whiskers and claws like they'd drunk a tub of werewolf (or I guess werecat) Miracle Gro. Their eyes went from golden brown to sharp green slits.

What on earth was ha—

Shut the front door, y'all. Wish number two is 'CATSSS', isn't it?

Sweet Boo giggled happily as she

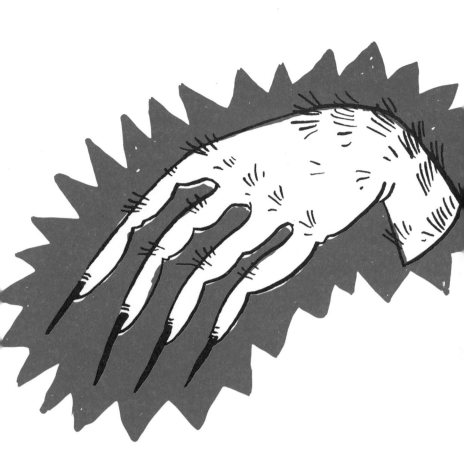

scooped up our new chonky three-
headed mascot and kissed their sweet
widdle noses.

chapter eleven

FROZEN TO THE BONE

Since the teacup debacle, and the cat shape-shifting hooplah, all the grown-ups left had been hyperventilating. If I wasn't so worried myself, watching their faces go from calm to purple panic might've been funny.

"The adults are being zippity-zero help," grumbled Bébé as she snacked dispiritedly on some passing pillbugs.

"I have now seen them fret, pace, curse and scowl," mumbled Mary. "All to no avail. I conclude none of them know what to do and they are all too old to admit it."

"Guuuys," whispered a strained Emmy LouLou. "I . . . I think I figured out

what wish number three is.
'COLD. AIR.' I was hoping
for a cool breeze, that's why I
wished it. All this fur in a heatwave.
I mean, come on! But . . . uh, I'm
not sure how to say this, but I think
whatever I touch turns to ice."

"No." I stepped up and patted her
on the back. "The Wishwind can't be
that off the mark. Are you sure . . . Oh,
I see." Both Emmy LouLou's parents
and Bébé's dad had stopped their
pacing. Not because they had come up
with a genius solution to get us out
of this mess, but because all three of
them were froze solid.

"DID YOU TURN MY FAMILY, THE HEAD LOA OF THE DEAD, INTO A PARENT POPSICLE?" screeched Bébé. She was puffing up in a towering rage.

At least it started out as anger, and then kept

on

going

and

growing.

Bébé started growing like a fifty-foot Thanksgiving Turkey Day parade float. Before anyone could blink, she had skyrocketed bigger than the swaying trees around us.

"Shoot, why did this go and happen to little ol' me?" boomed a very huge, very crabby Bébé. "I make one wish, y'all. One!

GROW. BIGGER.

Thinking if I was taller, Daddy might treat me with more respect. But nooo, now I'm just a giant undead Alice in Wonderland after she ate them messed-up mushrooms."

chapter twelve

I SCREAM, YOU SCREAM, WE ALL SCREAM FOR ICE CREAM BECAUSE THE WORLD IS BROKEN

I looked around.

There was only one adult left. My Maybe-Mom. And she was

smiling

like a gator who

just got her teeth whitened.

Even inside my

thoughts,

I couldn't call her *Mom*-Mom,
like a real one. I just couldn't.

"Remember, dear, dear children,"
cut in Maybe-Mom with the icy
composure of an overlooked
watermelon, "when our Lord Almighty
closes a screen door, he always
cracks open a window."

"But what if the door closes because a swarm of face-eating beetles wants to  get in? In that case, opening a window would be equally  catastrophic," suggested Mary.

Fair point, I thought.

"Mary, don't be foolish. Even carnivorous beetles have standards. As do I! This camp is clearly a death trap." She began fiddling with the long golden chain looped around her neck. My eyes were stuck like glue on her as she went on swinging the heavy pendant back

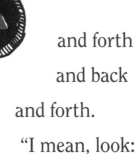

and forth
and back
and forth.

"I mean, look: teacups, cats and statues! This is unacceptable! So I am going to take my precious baby girl far away before any serious damage might befall her. There is always room at Our Lady of Perpetual Suffering and Misery for a new nun!"

"Take Lexie away?? Ma'am, please don't, I . . ." stumbled out Emmy LouLou.

At the same time I loudly protested, "I ain't going nowhere, no way no how!"

Before anyone else could speak up, Maybe-Mom ploughed on. "Young lady, I am your mother and I will take no more lip from you. Now, we've all had a long and trying day, and I want to put my feet up and drink a bottle of red. So off to bed with the lot of you!

I'll call social services first thing in the morning. They are always infinitely interested in a new batch of orphans. And Lexie, darling, start practising your prayers. Our nunnery awaits!"

DIAMONDS ARE A GIRL'S BEST FRIEND

We were all slumped around the cabin, trying to brainstorm our way out of this mess. Bébé couldn't quite fit inside any more, but nobody wanted to leave her out of the planning committee. So I cracked

open a window wide enough that
she could occasionally stick in her
big bony head. Look, only last week,
Mary had a mega

migraine so she
took her head
off for a while.
Literally. She
took it off and
tucked it into
bed. I screamed out loud the first few
times I saw her strutting around with
an empty neck. But, hey! I learned. I
adjusted.

But sitting here on my bed, stuck in
these awful thoughts, I didn't want to

learn or adjust. How could I adjust to a future without Grams?

Suddenly, Mary's jaw dropped. "Necklace!" she whispered into our sad sack silence.

I blinked, confused. Mary is sharp as a tack, maybe even sharper. No denying that, but how could a measly necklace fix our current situation?

"Don't give me that face! Look, it's a clue." And with that she daintily tilted her cup-dads so we could see what all the fuss was about. Inside the cups, at the very bottom in squishy tealeaf letters, the word n-e-c-k-l-a-c-e was spelled out.

Immediately, it sparked something in my imagination. I could feel one of my seriously awesome ideas starting to form right between my eyebrows.

"Question: do Wishwinds *live*

somewhere when they aren't being all Wishwindy?"

All I got was blank looks. (And believe me when I say a blank look on a bajillion-foot-tall skeleton is intense.)

"Come on, y'all," I pushed forward. "You know what I mean – like a genie! They get trapped in bottles, right? If a genie can come from a bottle, then what do Wishwinds get stuck in?"

More blank looks. Except for a teensy tiny lightbulb flickering on above Sweet Boo's head.

"NECKLACE!" whispered Sweet Boo.

"That's right, girlfriend. And most

importantly, who do we know who showed up today completely uninvited wearing a big chunky necklace around her nunny neck?"

"Your straight-up creepy mom!" hollered Bébé.

They were all catching on now, like a wildfire in July.

"Mhmm, my supposed mom, or whoever she really is." I let that idea sit in the air, before dropping the real bombshell. "Come on, we got us a necklace to steal."

LIAR LIAR
PANTS ON FIRE

A good deal later, after hours of scheming and building, a clock somewhere struck midnight. And underneath a blanket of swamp shadows, we snuck our way to the Visitors' cabin.

"Target is in sight. She seems to be . . ." whispered Emmy LouLou, her night-vision goggles straining. "Hey, wait, that's not your mom . . . Isn't that . . . NO!"

Quickly, I peered through my own goggles. I was expecting to see a nun (who may or may not be my mom) lying in the bunk far below with that bright shiny Wishwind necklace around her neck.

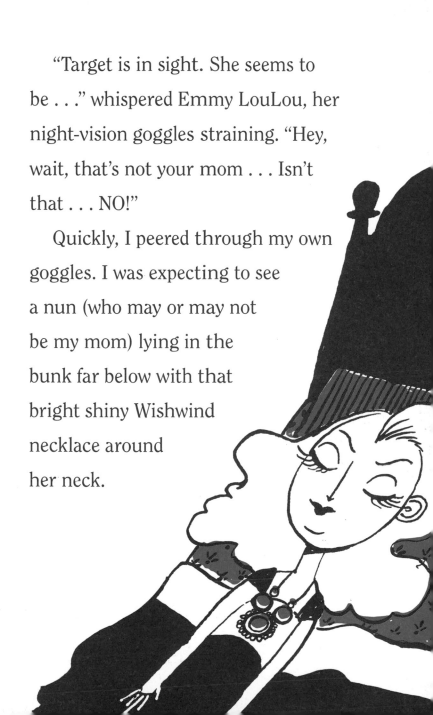

But what I saw instead was worse, way, way worse. It was **SCOUTMASTER EUPHEMIA VILE.**

That little yellow-bellied so and so! She was a liar liar pants on fire!

"Didn't we get rid of this germ once already?" asked Mary.

"You best hold me back, y'all, else I'm about to cancel this lady's birth certificate!" Bébé spat.

"Dadgummit," growled Sweet Boo.

This woman. Oh, this woman set a whole new level of low. What kind of person lies to a kid about being her mama? I was about to pitch me

a proper hissy fit, when Scoutmaster
Vile's eyes popped wide open . . .

chapter fifteen

IT'S SHOWTIME!

"**G**host Scouts, are you ready?" I screamed. They were.

Emmy LouLou and Mary pulled their bowstrings taut.

"FIRE!" I hollered.

And with a delicious whoosh-thump

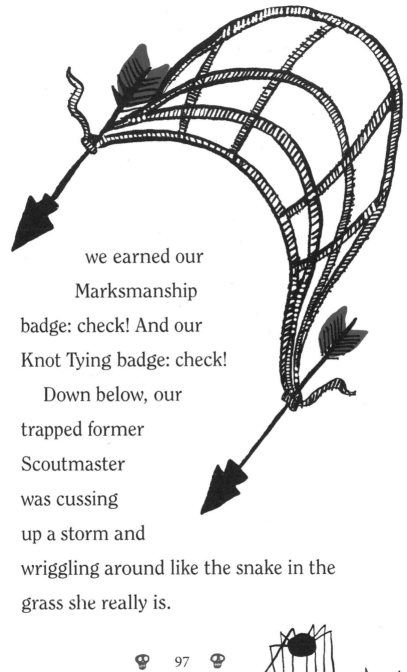

we earned our
Marksmanship
badge: check! And our
Knot Tying badge: check!
Down below, our
trapped former
Scoutmaster
was cussing
up a storm and
wriggling around like the snake in the
grass she really is.

Never fear, Sweet Boo
is here! First Aid badge:
check!

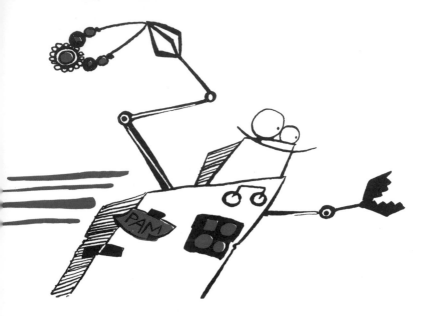

And with a bleep-bloop-bleep, we finished our mission off with the help of our handy-dandy newly built robot, Pam. (It was Mary's idea to build a robot with grabber claws perfect for necklace snatching. This way none of us accidentally touched the necklace – no one wanted to be responsible for more wishes.)

"Hello! My name is Pam. I am here to take your necklace. Give it to me or I will poke you ferociously until you do."

Okay, so Pam was a little overly enthusiastic about her job... But she got the job done nonetheless! With a snip and a snap she scooped up the cursed necklace.

Robotics badge: Checkcheckcheck!

Ghost Scouts for the win!

And that's when I heard the pounding coming from Scoutmaster Vile's closet . . .

chapter sixteen

HERE WE GO AGAIN

Leaping lizards! My heart just about jumped out of my throat.

What could possibly be so scary, so super deadly that even the wicked Scoutmaster Vile had to keep it locked up in her closet? We circled around the door, each of us clutching our makeshift weapons.

Thump! The beastie was clearly getting angrier as it slammed itself against the thin piece of door wood.

Thump!

Thump! On the bed behind us Scoutmaster Vile was rolling her eyes and trying to yell something through the bandaids.

THUMP!THUMP!THUMP!THUMP! Before my nerves could get the better of me, I twisted the handle and flung the door wide open.

Standing before me, in all her

golden years glory, was the answer to my wish. My wonderful Grams. Sure, she was angrier than a hornet in a maraca but that's only to be expected. You can't kidnap someone like my Grams and really think you'll get away with it!

"What in the blue blazes is going on here? A nun locked me in this closet, and there is a skeletal giantess in the sky. Lexie, if you don't come over here and give me a hug right this instant, I will blow a figurative gasket!"

I threw myself in her waiting arms and snuggled. That snuggle released all the emotions, and I started blubbering like a broken water spigot. I told her about Visitors' Weekend, the teacups, the monstrous impostor not-my-mom Euphemia Vile and most importantly about the Wishwind. She nodded and took it all in, with the occasional death glare at Scoutmaster

Vile. And just like that, she took charge.

"Young lady," she hollered up at our huge Bébé, "if I understand correctly, there is some kind of magical critter cooped up in this ratty pendant. And if you don't mind me saying, your wonderfully enormous feet look perfect for necklace stomping. Would you be so kind, and set this one free?"

"With pleasure, Miss Grams," laughed Bébé. Pam placed the necklace on the ground and with a resounding CRACK that made the air vibrate, Bébé crushed it under her mighty heel.

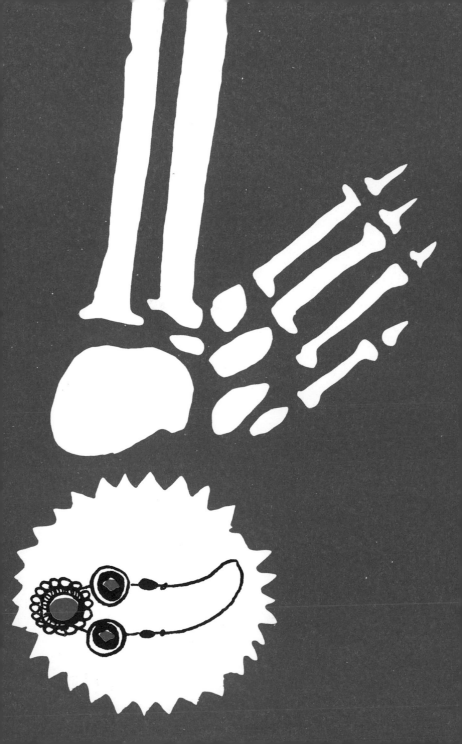

In a riot of laughter and freedom, the swamp exploded.

No, wait, wrong word.

It didn't literally explode. It blossomed.
It changed. All the wishes started
reversing faster than a stick of butter
melts in the microwave.

We had parents unfreezing, camp
counsellors de-furring and skeletal
systems shrinking all in the blink of a
cyclops' eye. Mary even got her dads
back to whole human.

Off in the distance, we heard a
happy sigh as the Wishwind dove
wild and free through the breeze.

"Thankssss amigossss!"

Everything was good in the world.

(Or at least, everything should have been good. It was Sweet Boo's idea to package Scoutmaster Vile up and ship her off to Wetonka. If we had known that she'd taken escapologist classes in school, we might've added some more tape!)

"WATCH YOUR BACKS, LITTLE GHOSTS, IT AIN'T OVER UNTIL I SAY IT'S OVER!"

GLOSSARY

A helpful section in any book that most people skip over, but you shouldn't.

Amphibians: small squishy animals that need some moisture to survive. Frogs, toads, salamanders and newts are all awesome amphibians.

Baron Samedi: the head Loa (spirit, see Loa below).

Cicadas: small bugs that scream their heads off; they sound like the whirring of an angry musical drill.

Cyclops: a giant creature from Greek and Roman mythology which has one large eye in the middle of its head.

Earwigging: secretly snooping and listening in on someone else's conversation.

Fishing Bobber: little red and white floaty balls that keep a fishing line from sinking too deeply.

Gasket: a tiny piece of rubber that seals pressure in car engines; the phrase "to blow a gasket" means to get real angry, or explode in grumpiness.

Hawaii: an amazing part of the world, made up of 137 islands located in the Pacific Ocean.

Hullabaloo: a loud uproar, a ruckus, a hoopla and all that.

Loa: the spirits of Louisiana Voodoo. While they are not gods themselves, they are treated with great respect and served in the hopes that the Loa will convey their prayers to God.

Miracle Gro: a type of plant fertilizer you can grab in the store that is supposed to make your plants grow extra super fast.

Scourge: someone or something that causes great and terrible trouble.

Turkey Day: another name for the
controversial American holiday,
'Thanksgiving'.

Wetonka: a town in South Dakota with
a population of eight people.

GHOST SCOUT EXTRAS

1. Ghost Scout hand sign:

Raise your paws and show some claws!

2. Ghost Scout pledge:

On my dishonour, I will try:

to serve whoever or whatever suits me,

to help the living and the dead at all

times, and to live by the Ghost

Scout Law.

3. Ghost Scout law:

I will do my best to be

honest and fair,

friendly-ish and helpful,

considerate and caring,

brush my fangs and shower occasionally,

be responsible for what I say and do,

and to

respect myself because I am awesome,

respect authority when they have earned

my respect,

use resources wisely,

make the world a stranger place,

and be a sibling to every Ghost Scout.

BIOGRAPHY:

Taylor Dolan was born into a house of stories and raised in Texas. Her mother used to read to her every night, and together they made their way through the worlds of Narnia, Oz and many more. Sometimes, when Taylor is feeling blue, her mother still reads to her and does the best voices for all the characters.

When she was younger she was a proud Girl Scout in Troop 809. During that time, she sold (and ate) many Girl Scout Cookies, camped down the street from an Emu farm, and learned the painful fish-flop method of re-entering a canoe after having been pushed in the water.

Many years later, she attended the Cambridge School of Art for her Master's Degree in Children's Book Illustration. She now lives in Arkansas, while using her imagination to pretend she still lives in Cambridge. This is her second written and illustrated book, and contains many little pieces of her heart.

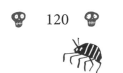

LEXIE WILDE thinks she's going to the Happy Hollow Camp for Joyful Boys and Girls. But Grams takes a wrong turn and they end up at Camp Croak, where Lexie discovers it's

much more fun sharing a cabin with a werewolf called Emmy LouLou, a fancy schmancy zombie called Mary Shelley and a baseball-cap-wearing ghost called Sweet Boo . . .

When the sickly-sweet Euphemia Vile appears and tries to take over, Lexie and her pals have to use all their talents (and badges) to thwart her wicked plans . . .

GUPPY BOOKS

Guppy Books is an independent children's publisher based in Oxford in the UK, publishing exceptional fiction for children of all ages. Small and responsive, inclusive and communicative, Guppy Books was set up in 2019 and publishes only the very best authors and illustrators from around the world.

From brilliantly funny illustrated tales for five-year-olds to inspiring and thought-provoking novels for young adults, Guppy Books promises to publish something for everyone. If you'd like to know more about our authors and books, go to the Guppy Aquarium on YouTube where you'll find interviews, drawalongs and all sorts of fun.

We hope that our books bring pleasure to young people of all ages, and also to the adults sharing these books with them. Children's literature plays a part in giving both young and old the resources and reflection needed to grow up in today's ever-changing world, and we hope that you enjoy this small piece of magic!

Bella Pearson
Publisher

www.guppybooks.co.uk